# حبة الذرة المحظوظة

# The lucky grain of corn

written and illustrated by Véronique Tadjo

Arabic translation by Ahmed Al-Hamdi

MILET

في قرية تقع في أعماق الغابة
كان يعيش أبٌ وأمٌ
وولدهما الوحيد سرور،
أعطوه حبة ذرة محظوظة.
أمسك سرور بالحبة في راحة يده
وأخذ ينظر اليها.
كانت حبة صغيرة جداً!

ترك سرور الحبة على صخرة.

In a village deep in the forest
Mother and Father gave
Soro, their only son,
a lucky grain of corn.
Soro held it in the palm of his hand
and looked at it.
It was so small!

He left it on a stone.

وفجأة،
خرجت من بين الأحراش جنيه بهيئة طير مسحور
وسرقت حبة الذرة المحظوظة
بنقرة واحدة من منقارها.

All of a sudden,
out of the bush came a guinea fowl
who stole the lucky grain of corn
with one peck of her beak.

كان والد سرور يعمل في حقله،
ووالدته منشغلة جداً.

Father was working on his farm.
Mother was very busy.

صار سرور يجري ويجري ويجري.

وكان الجو حاراً للغاية.
وكان سرور يتصبب عرقاً.
وكانت قدماه مغطاة بالرمل.
ولكن بالرغم من ذلك لم يتمكن من اللحاق بالطير المسحور!

ثم:


Soro ran and ran and ran.

It was terribly hot.
He was dripping with sweat.
His feet were covered in dust.
Yet he couldn't catch up with the fowl.

Then:

وصل سرور الى قرية
كانت تعيش فيها الأبقار .
فرحبت به الأبقار ترحيباً حاراً.
وقالت بقرة من بين الأبقار :
"إبقَ معنا أياماً قليلة،
وستكون صديقنا
وسوف نقدم لك كل ما لدينا من حليب."

ولكن سرور أجاب: "لا، لا، لا،
لابد لي من العثور على حبة الذرة المحظوظة!"
وصار يجري ويجري ويجري.

وكان الجو حاراً للغاية.
وكان سرور يتصبب عرقاً.
وكانت قدماه مغطاة بالرمل.
ولكن بالرغم من ذلك لم يتمكن من اللحاق
بالطير المسحور!
ثم:

Soro arrived in a village
where cows lived.
They gave him a warm welcome.
One of them said:
"Stay with us for a few days.
You will be our friend
and we shall give you all our milk."

But Soro replied:"No, no, no,
I must find my lucky grain of corn!"
He ran and ran and ran.

It was terribly hot.
He was dripping with sweat.
His feet were covered in dust.
Yet he couldn't catch up with
the fowl.

Then:

وصل سرور الى قرية ثانية
مليئة بالأكواخ الصغيرة الرائعة.
كان الأولاد والفتيات
في القرية يلعبون ويضحكون معاً.
وقالوا لسرور بصوت واحد:
"إبقَ معنا أياماً قليلة.
وسوف نقضّي وقتناً في اللعب هنا معاً.
إمسك بالكرة وانضم معنا في اللعب"!

ولكن سرور أجاب: "لا، لا، لا،
لابد لي من العثور على حبة الذرة المحظوظة!"،
وصار يجري ويجري ويجري.

Soro arrived in a second village
full of lovely little huts.
Boys and girls
were playing and laughing together.
They said with one voice:
"Stay with us for a few days.
Here we spend our time playing.
Catch the ball and join the game!"

But Soro replied: "No, no, no,
I must find my lucky grain of corn!"
He ran and ran and ran.

وكان الجو حاراً للغاية.
وكان سرور يتصبب عرقاً.
وكانت قدماه مغطاة بالرمل.
ولكن بالرغم من ذلك لم يتمكن من اللحاق
بالطير المسحور!

ثم:

It was terribly hot.
He was dripping with sweat.
His feet were covered in dust.
Yet he couldn't catch up with
the fowl.

Then:

وصل سرور الى قرية ثالثة.
مجموعة من الرجال كبار السن
لهم لحى بيضاء طويلة وكانوا يتحدثون مع بعضهم بعضاً
في ظل شجرة مانغو كبيرة.
ودعى أحد المسنين سروراً الى الجلوس
وقصّ له قصة جميلة.
وفي نهايتها قال له:
"إبقَ معنا أياماً قليلة.
نحن نعرف كثيراً من الحكايات
وسوف نعلمك
كيف تصبح ولداً حكيماً."

ولكن سرور نهض قائماً
وأجاب:"لا، لا، لا،
لابد لي من العثور على حبة الذرة المحظوظة!"

Soro arrived in a third village.
A group of elders
with long white beards were chatting
in the shade of a big mango tree.
One of them asked him to sit down
and told him a beautiful story.
At the end of it, he said:
"Stay with us for a few days.
We know lots of tales
and we shall teach you
how to become a wise boy."

But Soro stood up
and replied:"No, no, no,
I must find my lucky grain of corn!"

وصار يجري ويجري ويجري.
وكان الجو حاراً للغاية.
وكان سرور يتصبب عرقاً.
وكانت قدماه مغطاة بالرمل.
ولكن بالرغم من ذلك لم يتمكن من اللحاق
بالطير المسحور !

ثم:

He ran and ran and ran.
It was terribly hot.
He was dripping with sweat.
His feet were covered in dust.
Yet he couldn't catch up with
the fowl.

Then:

خرجت الجنية بهيئة الطير المسحور فجأة
وعبرت مساره.
قفز عليها ومسكها.
وصرخ قائلاً،
"لقد سرقت حبة الذرة المحظوظة مني.
أعيديها اليّ حالاً!"

ولكن الطير المسحور هزّ رأسه وقال:
"أنا متأسف جداً. لقد ابتلعتها.
وبدلاً عنها تمنى أمنية وسوف ألبيها لك!"

The guinea fowl
suddenly crossed his path.
He jumped and caught her.
"You have stolen my lucky grain of
corn," he screamed.
"Give it back to me at once!"

But the fowl shook her head and said:
"I am very sorry, I swallowed it.
In exchange, make a wish and I shall fulfil it!"

وهنا بدأ سرور يفكر تفكيراً شديداً.
وبعد مضي بعض الوقت، قال:
"كافة الناس الذين التقيت بهم وكافة الحيوانات التي مررت بها
حينما كنت أركض وراءك
كان من الممكن أن يصبحوا أصدقائي.
أتمنى أن أراهم ثانيةً!"

ومن ثم، وكأنه ضرب من السحر،
جاء كل فرد التقى به سرور وكل حيوان رآه هنا!
الأبقار وحليبها.
الأولاد والفتيات مع ألاعيبهم.
الرجال المسنون وقصصهم.

عندها لم تتمكن الجنيه التي ظهرت بهيئة طير مسحور
من الامساك عن الضحك
وظلت تضحك وتضحك.

So, Soro started thinking hard.
And after some time, he said:
"All the people and animals I met
while I was running after you
could have become my friends.
I wish I could see them again!"

And then, as if by magic,
everybody was there!
The cows with their milk.
The boys and girls with their games.
The elders with their stories.

And the guinea fowl
couldn't stop laughing.
Just couldn't stop laughing.

Other Véronique Tadjo titles by Milet:

Mamy Wata and the monster
Grandma Nana

**Milet Publishing Ltd**
PO Box 9916
London W14 0GS
England
Email: orders@milet.com
Website: www.milet.com

The lucky grain of corn / English – Arabic

First published in Great Britain by Milet Publishing Ltd in 2000
© Véronique Tadjo 2000
© Milet Publishing Ltd for English – Arabic 2000

ISBN 1 84059 275 3

We would like to thank Nouvelles Editions Ivoiriennes for the kind permission
to publish this dual language edition.

Designed by Catherine Tidnam and Mariette Jackson
Printed and bound in Belgium by Proost